A Treasure Cove Story

DISNEP FROZEN II

Adapted by	Illustrated by	Designed by
Nancy Cote	**Olga Mosqueda**	**Tony Fejeran**

This
Treasure Cove Story
belongs to

_____

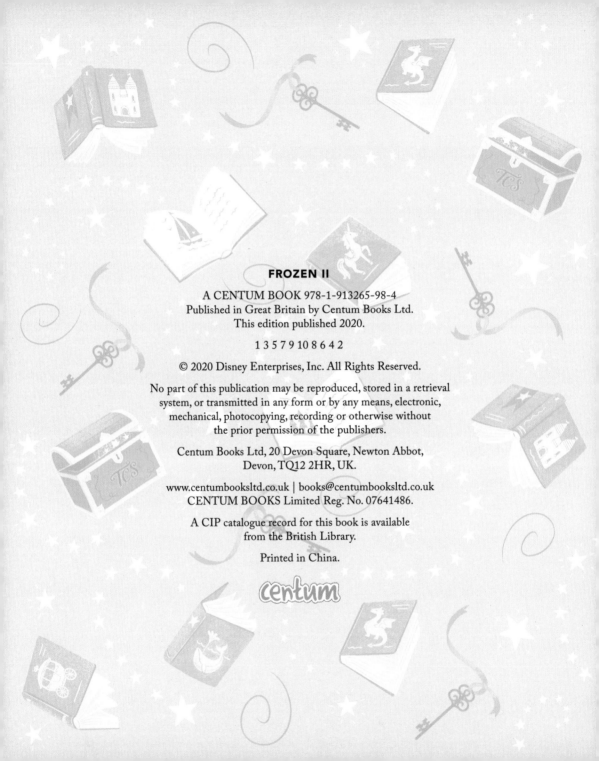

FROZEN II

A CENTUM BOOK 978-1-913265-98-4
Published in Great Britain by Centum Books Ltd.
This edition published 2020.

1 3 5 7 9 10 8 6 4 2

Centum Books Ltd, 20 Devon Square, Newton Abbot,
Devon, TQ12 2HR, UK.

www.centumbooksltd.co.uk | books@centumbooksltd.co.uk
CENTUM BOOKS Limited Reg. No. 07641486.

A CIP catalogue record for this book is available
from the British Library.

Printed in China.

centum

In the kingdom of Arendelle, Anna and Elsa loved the *lullaby* their mother sang to them when they were children.

The lullaby was about a **secret river**,
which held all the answers about the past.
It gave the girls a lot to think about and
excited their *imaginations*.

As time went on, Anna and Elsa grew older. Elsa discovered her magical power over **snow and ice**, which became stronger and stronger. One night, a **mysterious voice** called to her. What did it want?

Elsa realised that the
voice wanted her to travel
north. She went to the fjord
and shot out an enormous

icy blast!

It was clear that Elsa's magic had done something new and powerful.

But what did it mean?

The trolls rolled up to the cliffs to let
Elsa know that her blast had awakened
the spirits of the *Enchanted Forest*.

They warned her that the spirits were *angry*. The forest was also where a nomadic group of people called the *Northuldra* were said to live.

Elsa knew in her heart that she must follow the mysterious voice to the Enchanted Forest.

Anna and her friends Kristoff, Olaf and Sven went with Elsa. In the forest, they met the *Wind Spirit*, who whooshed around them.

They also met the Northuldra people, who told them **stories** and revealed that they were more **similar** to Elsa, Anna and their friends than they were **different**.

While Elsa and her friends were getting to know the Northuldra, the mighty **Fire Spirit** appeared and set the Enchanted Forest on fire!

Elsa tried to **stop** the spreading fire with her magic, but it wasn't working.

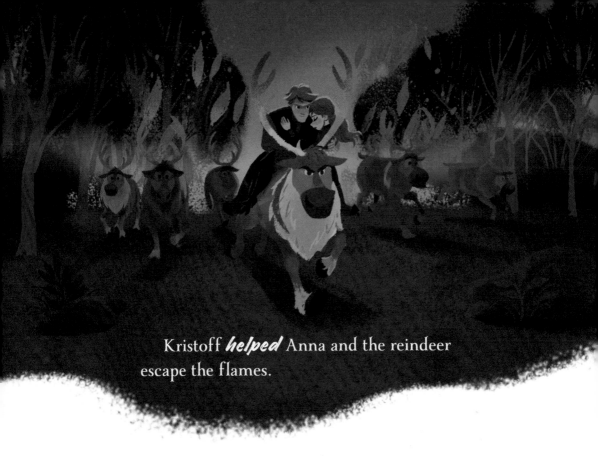

Kristoff *helped* Anna and the reindeer escape the flames.

Elsa was finally able to calm the Fire Spirit by feeding it *snowflakes*. The Fire Spirit was actually a little salamander.

Elsa heard the voice again, and she noticed that the Fire Spirit could hear it, too.

Elsa couldn't stay any longer. She had to continue her *journey*. Anna and Olaf joined her, while Kristoff and Sven stayed behind with the Northuldra.

Heading north, Anna and Elsa discovered their **_parents' shipwreck_**!

Inside the ship, they studied a map and learned that their parents had travelled north to understand why Elsa had magic.

Elsa feared losing Anna, just as she had lost their parents. Elsa decided to make the rest of the journey alone.

With a heavy heart, Elsa formed a boat made of ice that **scooped up** Anna and Olaf and carried **them safely away.**

Anna and Olaf loudly **protested**, but there was no way they could stop the boat after Anna accidentally steered it towards the sleeping **Earth Giants**. Anna and Olaf kept quiet as they passed them.

More determined than ever, Elsa reached the next part of her journey: the *Dark Sea*. Now she needed to cross it.

The **Water Nokk** reared up from the sea and tried to stop Elsa. After a fierce battle, Elsa and the Water Nokk realised that their powers were equal. A mutual respect formed between them.

Meanwhile, Anna and Olaf's journey continued into a cave, where an *ice sculpture* appeared in front of them. It was a signal from Elsa. The journey had answered some of the queen's questions.

Elsa had **_finally arrived_** in the north!
The voice that had called to her now quieted to a
whisper, and she realised it had been within her all
along. It had guided her to discover her inner peace.
By working together, the sisters were able
to restore peace and harmony to the land at last.

Treasure Cove Stories

Please contact Centum Books to receive the full list of titles in the *Treasure Cove Stories* series.
books@centumbooksltd.co.uk

Classic favourites

1 Three Little Pigs
2 Snow White and
the Seven Dwarfs
3 The Fox and the Hound
- Hide-and-Seek
4 Dumbo
5 Cinderella
6 Cinderella's Friends
7 Alice in Wonderland
8 Mad Hatter's Tea Party
from Alice in Wonderland
9 Mickey Mouse and
his Spaceship
10 Peter Pan
11 Pinocchio
12 Mickey and the Beanstalk
13 Sleeping Beauty
and the Good Fairies
14 The Lucky Puppy
15 Chicken Little
16 The Incredibles
17 Coco
18 Winnie the Pooh and Tigger
19 The Sword in the Stone
20 Mary Poppins
21 The Jungle Book
22 The Aristocats
23 Lady and the Tramp
24 Bambi
25 Bambi - Friends of the Forest

Recently published

50 Frozen
51 Cinderella is my Babysitter
52 Beauty and the Beast
- I am the Beast
53 Blaze and the Monster Machines
- Mighty Monster Machines
54 Blaze and the Monster Machines
- Dino Parade!
55 Teenage Mutant Ninja Turtles
- Follow the Ninja!
56 I am a Princess
57 The Big Book of Paw Patrol
58 Paw Patrol
- Adventures with Grandpa!
59 Paw Patrol - Pirate Pups!
60 Trolls
61 Trolls Holiday
62 The Secret Life of Pets
63 Zootropolis
64 Ariel is my Babysitter
65 Tiana is my Babysitter
66 Belle is my Babysitter
67 Paw Patrol
- Itty-Bitty Kitty Rescue
68 Moana
69 Nella the Princess Knight
- My Heart is Bright!
70 Guardians of the Galaxy
71 Captain America
- High-Stakes Heist!
72 Ant-Man
73 The Mighty Avengers
74 The Mighty Avengers
- Lights Out!
75 The Incredible Hulk
76 Shimmer & Shine
- Wish Upon a Sleepover
77 Shimmer & Shine - Backyard Ballet
78 Paw Patrol - All-Star Pups!
79 Teenage Mutant Ninja Turtles
- Really Spaced Out!
80 I am Ariel
81 Madagascar
82 Jasmine is my Babysitter
83 How to Train your Dragon
84 Shrek
85 Puss in Boots
86 Kung Fu Panda
87 Beauty and the Beast - I am Belle
88 The Lion Guard
- The Imaginary Okapi
89 Thor - Thunder Strike!
90 Guardians of the Galaxy
- Rocket to the Rescue!
91 Nella the Princess Knight
- Nella and the Dragon
92 Shimmer & Shine
- Treasure Twins!
93 Olaf's Frozen Adventure
94 Black Panther
95 Trolls
- Branch's Bunker Birthday
96 Trolls - Poppy's Party
97 The Ugly Duckling
98 Cars - Look Out for Mater!
99 101 Dalmatians
100 The Sorcerer's Apprentice
101 Tangled
102 Avengers
- The Threat of Thanos
103 Puppy Dog Pals
- Don't Rain on my Pug-Rade
104 Jurassic Park
105 The Mighty Thor
106 Doctor Strange

Latest publications

107 Captain Marvel
108 The Invincible Iron Man
109 Black Panther
- Warriors of Wakanda
110 The Big Freeze
111 Ratatouille
112 Aladdin
113 Aladdin - I am the Genie
114 Seven Dwarfs Find a House
115 Toy Story
116 Toy Story 4
117 Paw Patrol - Jurassic Bark!
118 Paw Patrol
- Mighty Pup Power!
119 Shimmer & Shine
- Pet Talent Show!
120 SpongeBob SquarePants
- Krabby Patty Caper
121 The Lion King - I am Simba
122 Winnie the Pooh
- The Honey Tree
123 Frozen II
124 Baby Shark and the
Colours of the Ocean
125 Baby Shark and
the Police Sharks!
126 Trolls World Tour

Book list may be subject to change.